AESOP'S FABLES

The Boy Who Cried Wolf

RETOLD BY MARY BERENDES • ILLUSTRATED BY NANCY HARRISON

Distributed by The Child's World®
1980 Lookout Drive • Mankato, MN 56003-1705
800-599-READ • www.childsworld.com

ACKNOWLEDGMENTS
The Child's World®: Mary Berendes, Publishing Director
The Design Lab: Art Direction and Design
Red Line Editorial: Editing

LIBRARY OF CONGRESS CATALOGING-IN-PUBLICATION DATA
Berendes, Mary.
  The boy who cried wolf / by Mary Berendes ; illustrated by Nancy Harrison.
    p. cm. — (Aesop's fables)
  Summary: A boy tending sheep on a lonely mountainside thinks it a fine joke
to cry "wolf" and watch the people come running, until the day a wolf is really
there and no one answers his call.
  ISBN 978-1-60253-524-4 (library bound : alk. paper)
  [1. Fables. 2. Folklore.] I. Harrison, Nancy, 1963- ill. II. Aesop. III. Title. IV. Series.
  PZ8.2.B46925Boy 2010
  398.2—dc22
  [E]   2010009973

Printed in the United States of America in Mankato, Minnesota.
July 2010
F11538

If you often lie, people won't believe you when you really *are* telling the truth.

There once was a shepherd boy. He often watched his sheep near a dark forest.

It was lonely and boring watching sheep all day. The only people nearby were farmers working in their fields.

One day, the boy thought of a way to have some fun. He ran toward the fields crying, "Wolf! Wolf!"

The farmers ran to help the boy. They searched and searched, but no wolf was found.

They stayed to talk with the
boy. They wanted to be sure
he and his flock were all right.
The boy liked this very much.

The next day, the boy tried
the same trick. He ran toward
the fields crying, "Wolf! Wolf!"
   Again, the farmers came
to help. Once again, they did
not find any wolf.

A few days later, a *real* wolf crept out of the dark forest. One by one, the wolf began to steal the shepherd's sheep.

The boy needed help! He ran toward the fields as fast as he could. He shouted loudly, "WOLF! WOLF!"

But the farmers, who had been fooled before, thought the boy was tricking them again. They did not come to help this time.

The hungry wolf had a very good meal.

AESOP

Aesop was a storyteller who lived more than 2,500 years ago. He lived so long ago, there isn't much information about him. Most people believe Aesop was a slave who lived in the area around the Mediterranean Sea—probably in or near the country of Greece.

Aesop's fables are known in almost every culture in the world, in almost every language. His fables are even *part* of some languages! Some common phrases come from Aesop's fables, such as "sour grapes" and "Never count your chickens before they've hatched."

ABOUT FABLES

Fables are one of the oldest forms of stories. They are often short and funny, and have animals as the main characters. These animals act like people. Often, fables teach the reader a lesson. This is called a *moral*. A moral might teach right from wrong, or show how to act in good, kind ways. A moral might show what happens when someone makes a poor decision. Fables teach us how to live wisely.

Mary Berendes has authored dozens of books for children, including nature titles as well as books about countries and holidays. She loves to collect antique books and has some that are almost 200 years old. Mary lives in Minnesota.

Nancy Harrison was born and raised in Montreal. She has worked as an art director, creative director, and advertising executive with clients all over the world. After relocating to Philadelphia, she began working as a freelance illustrator. Nancy's work has been published in dozens of magazines and over 30 children's books. Nancy currently lives in Vermont.